THE TOOTH FAIRY

VS.

SANTA

FOR MY SON NATHAN WHO INSPIRED ME TO
WRITE THIS STORY, AND HIS TOOTH FAIRY, BLUE, WHO BRINGS
MAGIC AND JOY TO OUR LIVES—JLBD

TO MY MUM, SHARON, WHO HAS INSTILLED IN ME A LIFELONG
PASSION FOR BOOKS, ART, AND STORYTELLING—EH

W

PENGUIN WORKSHOP
An Imprint of Penguin Random House LLC, New York

Visit us online at www.penguinrandomhouse.com.

Library of Congress Cataloging-in-Publication Data is available upon request.

ISBN 9781524790806   10 9 8 7 6 5 4 3 2 1

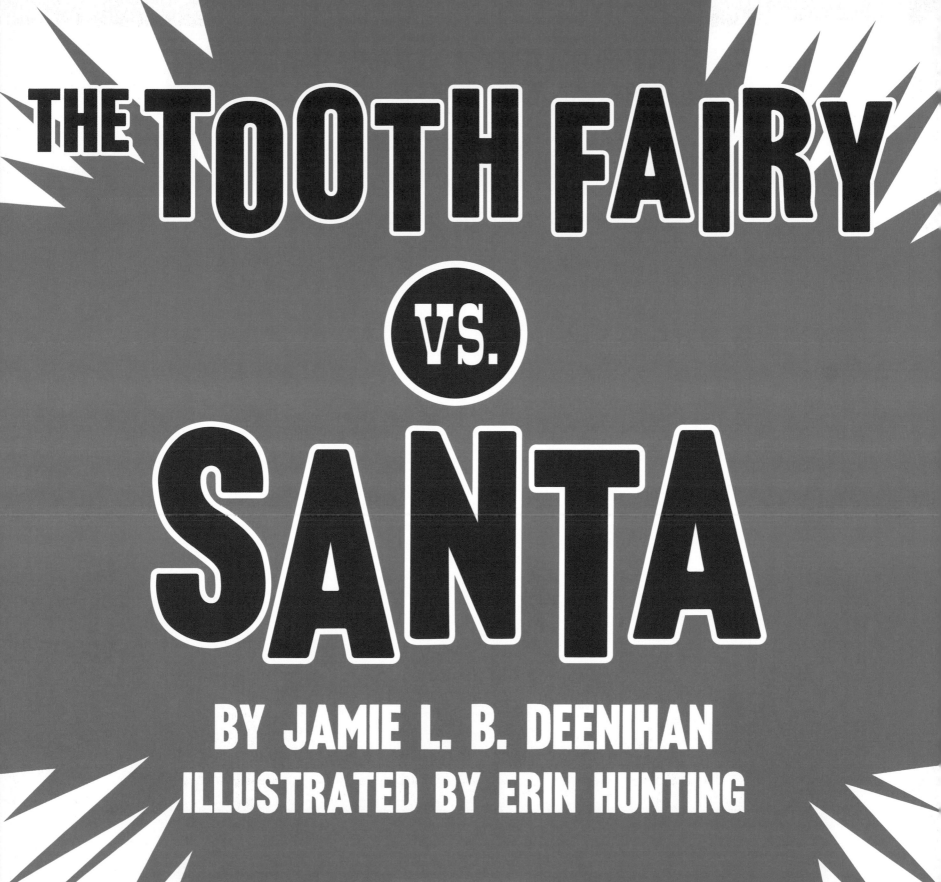

THE TOOTH FAIRY

VS.

SANTA

BY JAMIE L. B. DEENIHAN
ILLUSTRATED BY ERIN HUNTING

PENGUIN WORKSHOP

Blue had always dreamed of becoming the first fairy in his family to earn a spot on the Tooth Fairy Team.

While other young fairies in Toothtopia spent their free time at toothday parties, Blue was learning the names of teeth.

And when the others played brushball games, Blue practiced flying while carrying precious cargo, or trained at the Flitter Flutter Gym.

There wasn't much time for fun and friends, but when Blue arrived at the Tooth Fairy Command Center, he felt prepared to achieve what he'd worked so hard for.

Blue was the first fairy to submit his Tooth Fairy application.

Then, he aced the Tooth Fairy entrance exam . . .

. . . and passed the fitness tests with ease.

All he could do after that was wait to see if he'd be selected to take the final test that could earn him official Tooth Fairy status.

The next day, a letter from the
T. F. Command Center arrived.

Dear Blue,

As you know, only one fairy each year is selected to become a Tooth Fairy. After carefully reviewing your application, exam scores, and fitness test results, I'm pleased to inform you that you've been assigned case number 519822 for your final test. Locate and retrieve the client's lost tooth and deliver it back to the Command Center by midnight. If you are successful, you'll become a member of the Toothtopia Tooth Fairy Team. If not, you'll be assigned to the polishing department for one year.

May the floss be with you,
Mo Lars, TEO (Tooth Executive Officer)

Case Number:
519822
Name: Veda
Age: 5
Lost Tooth: Lower
Central Incisor
Address: 20 Tusks
Lane, Hopesville

Nobody wanted to work in the polishing department.

But Blue wasn't worried—he had prepared for this moment. What could go wrong?

He entered Veda's address into his Tooth Locator Device and was off!

There were many challenges in Blue's flight path . . .

. . . but finally, he arrived at his destination.

Blue couldn't fit through the keyhole, so he set his pixie-dust pen to the magic-door setting, drew a fairy-size entryway, and flew right in.

He was admiring the strange decorations when suddenly he heard a clatter coming from the chimney.

Blue cautiously took a closer look.

He saw rosy cheeks, a fluffy beard, and a perfect set of anterior teeth.

"You must be Veda's dad!" Blue shouted. "My name's Blue. I've been assigned to collect your daughter's lost tooth and leave this gift under her pillow."

"I'm not Veda's dad." Santa chuckled. "I'm Santa! And did you say gift? I'm the only one who leaves gifts on Christmas Eve."

"When is Christmas Eve?" Blue asked.

"Tonight!" Santa replied. "But please feel free to come back any other night of the year."

Blue checked his T. F. Handbook. "Sorry, Santa. It's company policy to collect a lost tooth on the same night that it falls out. There have been a few cases when that wasn't possible, but tonight is my final Tooth Fairy test, and I have to get back to the T. F. Command Center, with the tooth, by midnight!"

"We can't share Christmas Eve!" Santa insisted.

Blue was running out of time. "And I can't spend an entire year in the polishing department! There's only one way to settle this."

Blue switched his pixie-dust pen to the chalk setting to create a scoreboard.

"Winner stays," explained Blue.

"Loser leaves," Santa replied.

They shook hands and the competition began.

They lassoed,

they juggled,

and they fenced,

until they knocked over a plate of snacks and noticed Veda's letter.

Santa and Blue realized this night was about more than gifts or teeth.
It was about making Veda happy, and to do that, they needed to work as a team.

Santa cleaned while Blue decorated.

Blue collected Veda's tooth
while Santa delivered gifts.

And together, they wrote Veda a note.

Dear Veda,
Merry Christmas and congratulations on losing your first tooth! We had a busy night at your house delivering gifts, collecting your tooth, and becoming friends. We both loved your snacks and decorations! They made our visit to your house extra special.

Love,
Santa and your Tooth Fairy,
Blue

Blue was teaching Santa's reindeer some new tricks when he got an emergency reminder to return to the T. F. Command Center.

It would now be impossible for Blue to make it back in time.

Luckily, his new friend was able to help with that.

They reached the T. F. Command Center with just moments to spare. Blue wished Santa could stay, but he had many more deliveries to make before Christmas morning, so it was time to say goodbye.

Everyone at the T. F. Command Center was excited to hear about Blue's adventure.

Mo Lars presented him with an official Tooth Fairy Badge, along with a list of new clients.

And on his days off, Blue finally had time for fun and friends.

Everything was perfect.

Until Veda lost another tooth the night before Easter.

But Blue wasn't worried. What could go wrong?